To Ellie, Greg, Will & Baby K
With Love

Special Thanks to my family & my friends for their help & support.
In particular to Lucy at Lucy Tormey Visual Arts for her help &
encouragement as always. To Belvedere House, Gardens & Park and to
Cormac at Mind's i Graphic Design Ltd, for making the book possible.

Written & Illustrated by Dolores Keaveney
www.doloreskeaveney.com

Published by Mindsi

Design & Print by Mindsi Graphic Design Limited,

23 Marlinstown Park, Marlinstown, Mullingar, Co. Westmeath, Ireland.

www.mindsi.ie

Text copyright © Dolores Keaveney, 2010

Illustrations copyright © Dolores Keaveney, 2010

ISBN: 978-0-9562616-1-8

Jenny
the little
brown hen

Written & Illustrated by Dolores Keaveney
www.doloreskeaveney.com

Once upon a time there was a little brown hen called Jenny who lived at the bottom of Sean and Kathleen's garden. It was a beautiful garden with lots of lovely trees and flowers. There was plenty of room for her to run around. She loved to pick seeds and grass from the ground.

Every day **she** wandered up and down
under the hedges,
chatting with the little **robin** that
visited her sometimes. She also
had another visitor, the **busy**
bee, who came to collect
nectar from
the beautiful
foxgloves and
daisies that
grew in the
hedges.

She would sit down
and have a little rest
under the apple trees.
There was only
one problem. There
were no other hens or
roosters in this garden.
"I am very lonely,"
said Jenny,
to the little
robin and
to the busy bee.
She longed for the company
of other hens.

Sean made a little hen house for Jenny so that she could go inside when the weather was very bad or at nightime when she wanted to have a rest.

"This is a very **beautiful house,**"

she said to the
busy bee
and the **little robin.** "I am a very
lucky little hen, but I am very lonely indeed."

Sometimes two little children called Ellie and Greg would call to visit Jenny. They made her very happy. They would bring her bunches of lovely green grass which they had picked.

"How are you today?" they would ask.
"I am very well" Jenny would reply,
"but I am very lonely all
on my own."
Ellie and Greg loved to
visit this little hen
and to feed her.
Jenny chirped
and chuckled
with delight.
She loved the
company.

Greg said to Sean one day.

"Why is there no daddy with this little hen?"

Sean promised to get a new rooster to keep Jenny company.

Sure enough, a beautiful rooster arrived the next day.

His name was Sylvester.

He was a very strong and proud rooster
and he had golden brown feathers
that shone in the sunlight.

"Hello little hen," said the beautiful rooster "I have come to keep you company. My name is Sylvester."

"My name is Jenny," said the little hen. "I am so glad to see you."

They spent many hours chatting, chirping and walking around the lovely garden and having fun.

"Cluck, Cluck, Cluck, I am delighted you are here to keep me company," said Jenny to Sylvester "I am delighted to be here too," he replied.

Every morning Jenny would go to the corner of her little hen house and she would lay one very beautiful golden brown egg. She would cover it with straw to keep it safe.

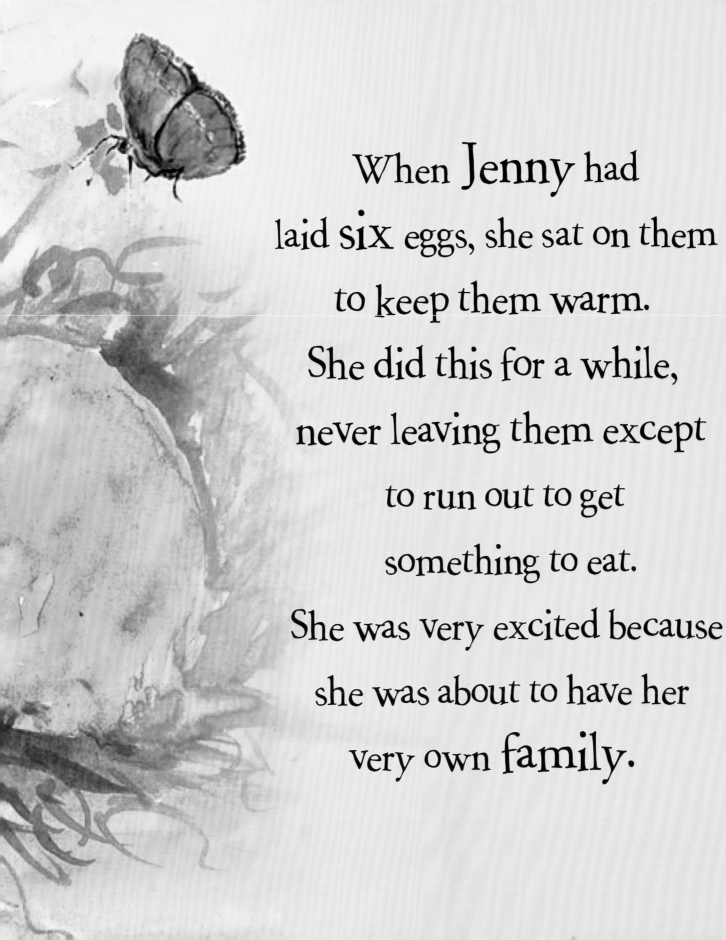

When Jenny had
laid six eggs, she sat on them
to keep them warm.
She did this for a while,
never leaving them except
to run out to get
something to eat.

She was very excited because
she was about to have her
very own family.

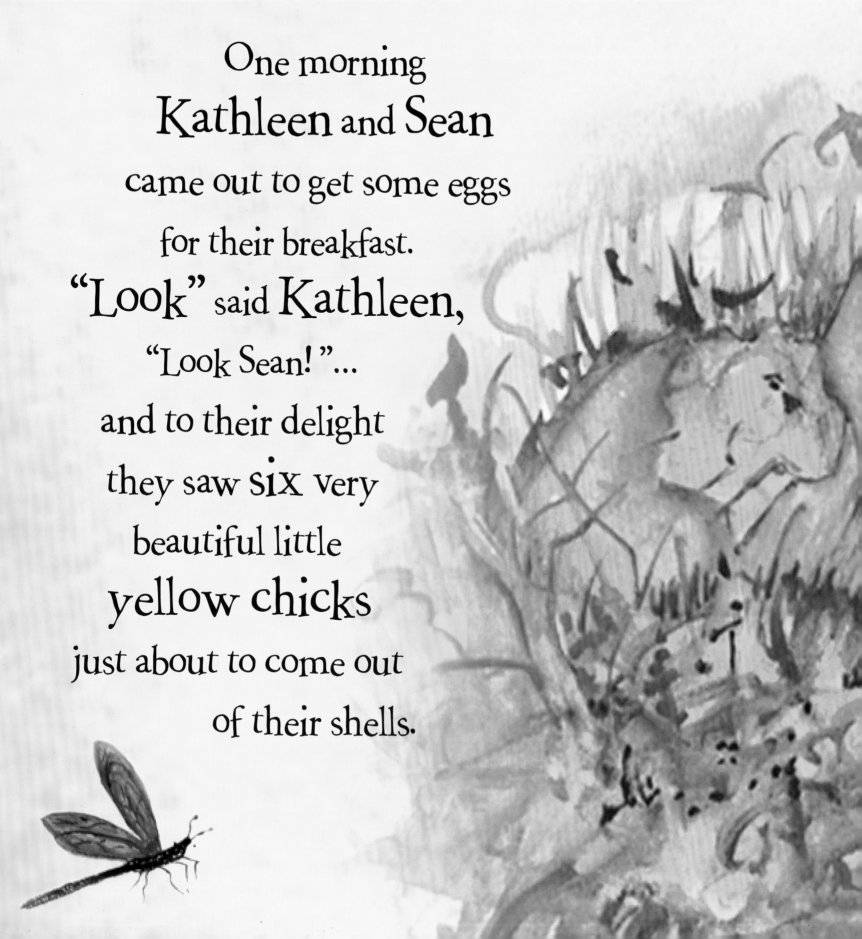

One morning
Kathleen and Sean
came out to get some eggs
for their breakfast.
"Look" said Kathleen,
"Look Sean!"...
and to their delight
they saw six very
beautiful little
yellow chicks
just about to come out
of their shells.

Soon the **six** little chicks were able to go out alone to pick grasses and to run around the garden. Then one day **Ellie** and **Greg** called with some food for **Jenny** the little brown hen. "Oh look," said **Ellie** to **Greg**, What a surprise!...

Dreamy   Cutie   Chirpy

They were filled with joy to see six little golden chicks running around. "What shall we call them?" said Ellie. They both thought for a while and then they said, "We will call them, Sweetie, Dreamy, Cutie, Chirpy, Cheeky and Hungry.

Sweetie

Cheeky

Hungry

When the chicks were big enough Jenny the hen and Sylvester the rooster took them out for a walk in the beautiful garden and to the poppy field nearby. They were very proud to show off their lovely new family.

Ellie and Greg were very happy too because they knew that Jenny had got her wish. She now had lots of company. She had Sylvester the rooster and her six little chicks. Ellie and Greg knew that Jenny the Little Brown Hen would never be lonely again.